People in bright clothes and funny hats strolled among the crowd. Some played funny-shaped guitars. Some tossed balls in the air. Some balanced swords on their hands.

Men and women dressed in capes and furs sat at long crowded wooden tables.

"I wonder which one is the knight," said Jack.

"I don't know," whispered Annie. "But they're eating with their fingers."

Suddenly, someone shouted behind them.

Look out for these other books in the
Magic Tree House series:

Dinosaurs Before Dark

Coming soon:

Mummies in the Morning
Pirates Past Noon

Join the Magic Tree House Club.
See back of book for details.

The Knight at Dawn

Mary Pope Osborne

Illustrated by Sal Murdocca

SCHOLASTIC

For Nathaniel Pope

Scholastic Children's Books,
Commonwealth House, 1–19 New Oxford Street,
London WC1A 1NU, UK
a division of Scholastic Ltd
London ~ New York ~ Toronto ~ Sydney ~ Auckland
Mexico City ~ New Delhi ~ Hong Kong

Published by arrangement with Random House Children's Books,
a division of Random House Inc.
First published in the UK by Scholastic Ltd, 2000

ISBN 0 439 01453 0

Typeset by Rowland Phototypesetting Ltd,
Bury St Edmunds, Suffolk
Printed by Cox & Wyman Ltd,
Reading, Berkshire

3 5 7 9 10 8 6 4 2

Contents

1
The Dark Woods

Jack couldn't sleep.

He put his glasses on. He looked at the clock. Five-thirty.

Too early to get up.

Yesterday so many strange things had happened. Now he was trying to figure them out.

He turned on the light. He picked up his notebook. He looked at the list he'd made before going to bed.

found tree house in woods

found lots of books in it

pointed to Pteranodon picture in book

made a wish

went to time of dinosaurs

pointed to picture of Frog Creek

woods

made a wish

came home to Frog Creek

Jack pushed his glasses into place. Who
was going to believe any of this?

Not his mum. Or his dad. Or his third-grade teacher, Miss Watkins. Only his seven-year-old sister, Annie. She'd gone with him to the time of the dinosaurs.

"Can't you sleep?"

It was Annie, standing in his doorway.

"Nope," said Jack.

"Me neither," said Annie. "What are you doing?"

She walked over to Jack and looked at his notebook. She read the list.

"Aren't you going to write about the gold medal?" she asked.

"You mean the gold medallion," said Jack.

He picked up his pencil and wrote:

found this in dinosaur time

"Aren't you going to put the letter M on the medal?" said Annie.

"Medallion," said Jack. "Not medal."

He added an M:

"Aren't you going to write about the magic person?" said Annie.

"We don't know for sure if there is a magic person," said Jack.

"Well, someone built the tree house in the woods. Someone put the books in it. Someone lost a gold medal in dinosaur time."

"Medallion!" said Jack for the third time. "And I'm just writing the facts. The stuff we know for sure."

"Let's go back to the tree house right now," said Annie, "and find out if the magic person is a fact."

"Are you mad?" said Jack. "The sun's

not even up yet."

"Come on," said Annie. "Maybe we can catch them sleeping."

"I don't think we should," said Jack. He was worried. What if the "magic person" was mean? What if he or she didn't want kids to know about the tree house?

"Well, I'm going," said Annie.

Jack looked out of his window at the dark grey sky. It was almost dawn.

He sighed. "Okay. Let's get dressed. I'll meet you at the back door. Be quiet."

"Brilliant!" whispered Annie. She tiptoed away as quietly as a mouse.

Jack put on jeans, a warm sweatshirt, and trainers. He tossed his notebook and pencil in his rucksack.

He crept downstairs.

Annie was waiting by the back door. She shone a torch in Jack's face. "Ta-da! A magic wand!" she said.

"Shhh! Don't wake up Mum and Dad," whispered Jack. "And turn that torch off. We don't want anyone to see us."

Annie nodded and turned it off. Then she clipped it on to her belt.

They slipped out of the door into the cool early-morning air. Crickets were chirping. The dog next door barked.

"Quiet, Henry!" whispered Annie.

Henry stopped barking. Animals always seemed to do what Annie said.

"Let's run!" said Jack.

They dashed across the dark wet lawn and didn't stop until they reached the woods.

"We need the torch now," said Jack.

Annie took it off her belt and switched it on.

Step by step, she and Jack walked between the trees. Jack held his breath. The dark woods were scary.

"Gotcha!" said Annie, shining the

torch in Jack's face.

Jack jumped back. Then he frowned.

"Don't do that!" he said.

"I scared you," said Annie.

Jack glared at her.

"Stop pretending!" he whispered. "This is serious."

"Okay, okay."

Annie shone her torch over the tops of the trees.

"Now what are you doing?" said Jack.

"Looking for the tree house!"

The light stopped moving.

There it was. The mysterious tree house. At the top of the tallest tree in the woods.

Annie shone her light at the tree house, and then down the tall ladder. All the way to the ground.

"I'm going up," she said. She gripped the torch and began to climb.

"Wait!" Jack called.

What if someone was in the tree house?

"Annie! Come back!"

But she was gone. The light disappeared. Jack was alone in the dark.

2

Leaving Again

"No one's here!" Annie shouted down.

Jack thought about going home. Then he thought about all the books in the tree house.

He climbed up the ladder. When he was nearly at the tree house, he saw light in the distant sky. Dawn was starting to break.

He crawled through a hole in the floor and took off his rucksack.

It was dark inside the tree house.

Annie was shining her torch on the books scattered about.

"They're still here," she said.

She stopped the light on a dinosaur book. It was the book that had taken them to the time of the dinosaurs.

"Remember the Tyrannosaurus?" asked Annie.

Jack shuddered. Of course he remembered! How could anyone forget seeing a real live Tyrannosaurus rex?

The light fell on a book about Pennsylvania. A red silk bookmark stuck out of it.

"Remember the picture of Frog Creek?" said Annie.

"Of course," said Jack. That was the picture that had brought them home.

"There's my favourite," said Annie.

The light was shining on a book about knights and castles. There was a blue leather bookmark in it.

Annie turned to the page with the bookmark. There was a picture of a knight on a black horse. He was riding towards a castle.

"Annie, close that book," said Jack. "I know what you're thinking."

Annie pointed at the knight.

"Don't, Annie!"

"We wish we could see this knight for real," Annie said.

"No, we don't!" shouted Jack.

They heard a strange sound.

"*Neeee-hhhh!*"

It sounded like a horse neighing.

They both went to the window.

Annie shone the torch down on the ground.

"Oh no," whispered Jack.

"A knight!" said Annie.

A knight in shining armour! Riding a black horse! Through the Frog Creek woods!

Then the wind began to moan. The leaves began to tremble.

It was happening again.

"We're leaving!" cried Annie. "Get down!"

The wind moaned louder. The leaves shook harder.

And the tree house started to spin. It spun faster and faster!

Jack squeezed his eyes shut.

Then everything was still.

Absolutely still.

Jack opened his eyes. He shivered. The air was damp and cool.

The sound of a horse's whinny came again from below.

"*Neeee-hhhh!*"

"I think we're here," whispered Annie. She was still holding the castle book.

Jack peeked out of the window.

A huge castle loomed out of the fog.

He looked round. The tree house was in a different oak tree. And down below, the knight on the black horse was riding by.

"We can't stay here," said Jack. "We have to go home and make a plan first." He picked up the book about Pennsylvania. He opened it to the page with the red silk bookmark. He pointed to the photograph of the Frog Creek woods. "I wish—"

"No!" said Annie. She pulled the book away from him. "Let's stay! I want to visit the castle!"

"You're mad. We have to examine the situation," said Jack. "From home."

"Let's examine it here!" said Annie.

"Come on." He held out his hand. "Give it."

Annie gave Jack the book. "Okay. You can go home. I'm staying," she said. She clipped the torch to her belt.

"Wait!" said Jack.

"I'm going to take a peek. A teeny peek," she said. And she scooted down the ladder.

Jack groaned. Okay, she had won. He couldn't leave without her. Besides, he sort of wanted to take a peek himself.

He put down the book about Pennsylvania.

He dropped the castle book into his rucksack. He stepped on to the ladder. And headed down into the cool misty air.

3

Across the Bridge

Annie was under the tree, looking across the foggy ground.

"The knight's riding towards that bridge, I think," said Annie. "The bridge goes to the castle."

"Wait. I'll look it up," said Jack. "Give me the torch!"

He took the torch from her and pulled the castle book out of his rucksack. He opened it to the page with the leather bookmark.

He read the words under the picture of the knight:

This is a knight arriving for a castle feast. Knights wore armour when they travelled long and dangerous distances. The armour was very heavy. A helmet alone could weigh up to eighteen kilos.

Wow! Jack had weighed eighteen kilos when he was five years old. So it'd be like riding a horse with a five-year-old on your head.

Jack pulled out his notebook. He wanted to take notes, as he'd done on their dinosaur trip.

He wrote:

heavy head

What else?

He turned the pages of the castle

book. He found a picture that showed the whole castle and the buildings around it.

"The knight's crossing the bridge," said Annie. "He's going through the gate. . . He's gone."

Jack studied the bridge in the picture. He read:

> A drawbridge crossed the moat. The moat was filled with water, to help protect the castle from enemies. Some people believe crocodiles were kept in the moat.

Jack wrote in his notebook:

crocodiles in moat?

"Look!" said Annie, peering through the mist. "A windmill! Right over there!"

"Yeah, there's a windmill in here, too," said Jack, pointing at the picture.

"Look at the *real* one, Jack," said Annie. "Not the one in the book."

A piercing shriek split the air.

"Yikes," said Annie. "It sounded like it came from that little house over there!" She pointed through the fog.

"There's a little house *here*," said Jack, studying the picture. He turned the page and read:

> *The hawk house was in the inner ward of the castle. Hawks were trained to hunt other birds and small animals.*

Jack wrote in his notebook:

hawks in hawk house

"We must be in the inner ward," said Jack.

"Listen!" whispered Annie. "You hear

that? Drums! Horns! They're coming from the castle. Let's go and see."

"Wait," said Jack. He turned more pages of the book.

"I want to see what's *really* going on, Jack. Not what's in the book," said Annie.

"But look at this!" said Jack.

He pointed to a picture of a big party. Men were standing by the door, playing drums and horns.

He read:

> *Fanfares were played to announce different dishes in a feast. Feasts were held in the Great Hall.*

"You can look at the book. I'm going to the real feast," said Annie.

"Wait," said Jack, studying the picture. It showed boys his age carrying trays of food. Whole pigs. Pies. Peacocks with all their feathers. *Peacocks?*

Jack wrote:

they eat peacocks?

He held up the book to show Annie. "Look, I think they eat. . ."

Where was she? Gone. Again.

Jack looked through the fog.

He heard the real drums and the real horns. He saw the real hawk house, the real windmill, the real moat.

He saw Annie dashing across the real drawbridge. Then she vanished through the gate leading to the castle.

4

Into the Castle

"I'm going to kill her," muttered Jack.

He threw his stuff into his rucksack and moved towards the drawbridge. He hoped no one would see him.

It was getting darker. It must be night.

When he got to the bridge, he walked across. The wooden planks creaked under his feet.

He peered over the edge of the

bridge. Were there any crocodiles in the moat?

He couldn't tell.

"Halt!" someone shouted. A guard on top of the castle wall was looking down.

Jack dashed across the bridge. He ran through the castle gate and into the courtyard.

From inside the castle came the sounds of music, shouting and laughter.

Jack hurried to a dark corner and crouched down. He shivered as he looked around for Annie.

Flaming torches lit the high wall around the courtyard. The courtyard was nearly empty.

Two boys led horses that clopped over the grey cobblestones.

"*Neeee-hhhh!*"

Jack turned. It was the knight's black horse!

"Psssst!"

He peered into the darkness.

There was Annie.

She was hiding behind a well in the centre of the courtyard. She waved at him.

Jack waved back. He waited till the boys and horses disappeared inside the stable. Then he dashed to the well.

"I'm going to find the music!" whispered Annie. "Are you coming?"

"Okay," Jack said with a sigh.

They tiptoed together across the cobblestones. Then they slipped into the entrance of the castle.

Noise and music came from a bright room in front of them. They stood on one side of the doorway and peeked in.

"The feast in the Great Hall!" whispered Jack. He held his breath as he stared in awe.

A giant fireplace blazed at one end of the noisy room. Antlers and rugs hung on the stone walls. Flowers covered the floor. Boys in short dresses carried huge trays of food.

Dogs were fighting over bones under the tables.

People in bright clothes and funny hats strolled among the crowd. Some played funny-shaped guitars. Some tossed balls in the air. Some balanced swords on their hands.

Men and women dressed in capes and furs sat at long crowded wooden tables.

"I wonder which one is the knight," said Jack.

"I don't know," whispered Annie. "But they're eating with their fingers."

Suddenly, someone shouted behind them.

Jack whirled around.

A man carrying a tray of pies was

standing a few metres away.

"Who art thou?" he asked angrily.

"Jack," squeaked Jack.

"Annie," squeaked Annie.

Then they ran as fast as they could down a dimly-lit hallway.

5

Trapped

"Come on!" cried Annie.

Jack raced behind her.

Were they being followed?

"Here! Quick!" Annie dashed towards a door off the hallway. She pushed the door open. The two of them stumbled into a dark cold room. The door creaked shut behind them.

"Give me the torch," said Annie. Jack handed it to her, and she switched it on.

Yikes! A row of knights right in front of them!

Annie flicked off the light.

Silence.

"They aren't moving," Jack whispered.

Annie turned the light back on.

"They're just suits," Jack said.

"Without heads," said Annie.

"Let me have the torch a second," said Jack, "so I can look in the book."

Annie handed him the torch. He pulled out the castle book. He flipped through the pages until he found what he was looking for.

Jack put the book away. "It's called the armoury," he said. "It's where armour and weapons are stored."

He shone the torch around the room.

"Oh, cool," whispered Jack.

The light fell on shiny breastplates, leg plates, arm plates. On shelves filled with helmets and weapons. On shields, spears, swords, crossbows, clubs, battle-axes.

There was a noise in the hall. Voices!

"Let's hide!" said Annie.

"Wait," said Jack. "I've got to check on something first."

"Hurry," said Annie.

"It'll take just a second," said Jack. "Hold this." He handed Annie the torch.

He tried to lift a helmet from a shelf. It was too heavy.

He bent over and dragged the helmet over his head. The visor slammed shut.

Oh, forget it. It was *worse* than having a five-year-old on your head. More like having a ten-year-old on your head.

Not only could Jack not lift his head, he couldn't see anything, either.

"Jack!" Annie's voice sounded far away. "The voices are getting closer!"

"Turn off the torch!" Jack's voice echoed inside the metal chamber.

He struggled to get the helmet off.

Suddenly he lost his balance and went crashing into other pieces of armour.

The metal plates and weapons clattered to the floor.

Jack lay on the floor in the dark.

He tried to get up. But his head was too heavy.

He heard deep voices.

Someone grabbed him by the arm. The next thing he knew, his helmet was pulled off. He was staring into the blazing light of a fiery torch.

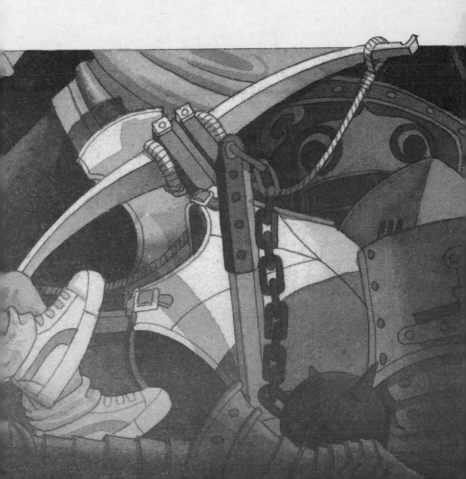

6

Ta~da!

In the torchlight, Jack saw three huge men standing over him.

One with very squinty eyes held the torch. One with a very red face held Jack. And one with a very long moustache held on to Annie.

Annie was kicking and yelling.

"Stop!" said the one with the very long moustache.

"Who art thou?" said the one with the

very red face.

"Spies? Foreigners? Egyptians? Romans? Persians?" said the squinty-eyed one.

"No, you idiots!" said Annie.

"Oh, great," Jack muttered.

"Arrest them!" said Red-face.

"The dungeon!" said Squinty-eyes.

The guards marched Jack and Annie out of the armoury. Jack looked back frantically. Where was his rucksack?

"Go!" said a guard, giving him a push.

Jack went.

Down they marched, down the long dark hallway. Squinty, Annie, Moustache, Jack and Red.

Down a narrow winding staircase.

Jack heard Annie shouting at the guards. "Idiots! Meanies! We didn't do anything!"

The guards laughed. They didn't take her seriously at all.

At the bottom of the stairs was a big

iron door with a bar across it.

Squinty pushed the bar off the door. Then he shoved at the door. It creaked open.

Jack and Annie were pushed into a cold clammy room.

The fiery torch lit the dungeon. There were chains hanging from the filthy walls. Water dripped from the ceiling, making puddles on the stone floor. It was the creepiest place Jack had ever seen.

"We'll keep them here till the feast is done. Then turn them over to the duke," said Squinty. "He knows how to take care of thieves."

"There will be a hanging tomorrow," said Moustache.

"If the rats don't get them first," said Red.

They all laughed.

Jack saw that Annie had his rucksack. She was quietly unzipping it.

"Come on, let's chain the two of 'em," said Squinty.

The guards moved towards them. Annie whipped her torch out of the rucksack.

"Ta-da!" she yelled.

The guards froze. They stared at the shiny electric torch in her hand.

Annie switched the light on. The guards gasped in fear. They jumped back against the wall.

Squinty dropped his fiery torch. It fell into a dirty puddle on the floor, sputtered, and went out.

"My magic wand!" Annie said, waving the torch. "Get down or I'll wipe you out!"

Jack's mouth dropped open.

Annie fiercely pointed her light at one, then the other. Each howled and covered his face.

"Down! All of you! Get down!" shouted Annie.

One by one, the guards lay down on the wet floor.

Jack couldn't believe it.

"Come on," Annie said to him. "Let's go."

Jack looked at the open doorway. He looked at the guards quaking on the ground.

"Hurry!" said Annie.

In one quick leap, Jack followed her out of the terrible dungeon.

7

A Secret Passage

Annie and Jack raced back up the winding stairs and down the long hallway.

They hadn't gone far when they heard shouting behind them.

Dogs barked in the distance.

"They're coming!" Annie cried.

"In here!" said Jack. He shoved open a door off the hallway and pulled Annie into a dark room.

Jack pushed the door shut. Then Annie shone her torch around the room. There were rows of sacks and wooden barrels.

"I'd better look in the book," said Jack. "Give it to me!"

Annie gave him the torch and his rucksack. He pulled out the book and started tearing through it.

"Shhh!" said Annie. "Someone's coming."

Jack and Annie jumped behind the door as it creaked open.

Jack held his breath. A light from a flaming torch danced wildly over the sacks and barrels.

The light disappeared. The door slammed shut.

"No way," whispered Jack. "We have to hurry. They might come back."

His hands were trembling as he flipped through the pages of the castle book.

"Here's a map of the castle," he said. "Look, this must be the room we're in. It's a storeroom." Jack studied the room in the book. "These are sacks of flour and barrels of wine."

"Who cares? We have to go!" said Annie. "Before they come back!"

"No. Look," said Jack. He pointed at the map. "Here's a trapdoor."

He read aloud:

"This door leads from the storeroom through a secret passage to a precipice over the moat."

"What's a precipice?" said Annie.

"I don't know. We'll find out," said Jack. "But first we have to find the door."

Jack looked at the picture carefully. Then he shone the torch around the room.

The floor of the room was made up of

stones. The trapdoor in the picture was five stones away from the door to the hall.

Jack shone the light on the floor and counted the stones. "One, two, three, four, five."

He stamped on the fifth stone. It was loose!

He put the torch on the floor. He worked his fingers under the thin sheet of stone and tried to lift it.

"Help," Jack said.

Annie came over and helped him lift the stone square out of its place. Underneath was a small wooden door.

Jack and Annie tugged on the rope handle of the door. The door fell open with a thunk.

Jack picked up the torch and shone it on the hole.

"There's a little ladder," he said. "Let's go!"

He clipped on the torch and felt his way down the small ladder. Annie followed.

When they both reached the bottom of the ladder, Jack shone the light around them.

There was a tunnel!

He crouched down and began moving through the damp creepy tunnel. The torch barely lit the stone walls.

He shook the light. Were the batteries running down?

"I think our light's dying!" he said to Annie.

"Hurry!" she called from behind.

Jack went faster. His back hurt from crouching.

The light got dimmer and dimmer.

He was desperate to get out of the castle before the batteries died completely.

Soon he reached another small

wooden door. The door at the end of the tunnel!

Jack unlatched the door and pushed it open.

He poked his head outside.

He couldn't see anything in the misty darkness.

The air felt good. Cool and fresh. He took a deep breath.

"Where are we?" whispered Annie behind him. "What do you see?"

"Nothing. But I think we've come to the outside of the castle," said Jack. "I'll find out."

Jack put the torch in his rucksack. He put the sack on his back. He stuck his hand out of the door. He couldn't feel the ground. Just air.

"I'm going to have to go feet first," he said.

Jack turned around in the small tunnel. He lay down on his stomach.

He stuck one leg out of the door. Then the other.

Jack inched down, bit by bit, until he was hanging out of the door, clinging to the ledge.

"This must be the precipice!" he called to Annie. "Pull me up!"

Annie reached for Jack's hands. "I can't hold you!" she said.

Jack felt his fingers slipping. Then down he fell.

Down through the darkness.

SPLASH!

8
The Knight

Water filled Jack's nose and covered his head. His glasses fell off. He grabbed them just in time. He coughed and flailed his arms.

"Jack!" Annie was calling from above.

"I'm in . . . the moat!" said Jack, gasping for air. He tried to tread water and put his glasses back on. With his rucksack, his trainers, and his heavy clothes, he could hardly stay afloat.

SPLASH!

"Hi! I'm here!" Annie sputtered.

Jack could hear her nearby. But he couldn't see her.

"Which way's land?" Annie asked.

"I don't know! Just swim!"

Jack dog-paddled through the cold black water.

He heard Annie swimming, too. At first it seemed as if she was swimming in front of him. But then he heard a splash behind him.

"Annie?" he called.

"What?" Her voice came from in front. Not behind.

Another splash. *Behind.*

Jack's heart almost stopped. Crocodiles? He couldn't see anything through his water-streaked glasses.

"Annie!" he whispered.

"What?"

"Swim faster!"

"But I'm here! I'm over here! Near the edge!" she whispered.

Jack swam through the dark towards her voice. He imagined a crocodile slithering after him.

Another splash! Not far away!

Jack's hand touched a wet live thing.

"*Ahhhh!*" he cried.

"It's me! Take my hand!" said Annie.

Jack grabbed her hand. She pulled him to the edge of the moat. They crawled over an embankment on to the wet grass.

Safe!

Another splash came from the moat waters.

"Oh, great," Jack said.

He was shivering all over. His teeth were chattering. He shook the water off his glasses and put them back on.

It was so misty he couldn't see the castle. He couldn't even see the moat, much less a crocodile.

"We . . . we made it," said Annie. Her teeth were chattering, too.

"I know," said Jack. "But where are we?" He peered at the foggy darkness.

Where was the drawbridge? The windmill? The hawk house? The grove of trees? The tree house?

Everything had been swallowed up by the thick soupy darkness.

Jack reached into his wet rucksack and pulled out the torch. He pushed the switch. No more light.

They were trapped. Not in a dungeon, but in the still cold darkness.

"*Neeee-hhhh!*"

A horse's whinny.

Just then the clouds parted. A full moon was shining in the sky. A pool of

light spread through the mist.

Then Jack and Annie saw him just a few metres away. The knight.

He sat on the black horse. His armour shone in the moonlight. A visor hid his face. But he seemed to be staring straight at Jack and Annie.

9

Under the Moon

Jack froze.

"It's him," Annie whispered.

The knight held out his gloved hand.

"Come on, Jack," Annie said.

"Where are you going?" said Jack.

"He wants to help us," said Annie.

"How do you know?"

"I can just tell," said Annie.

Annie stepped towards the horse. The knight dismounted.

The knight picked Annie up and put her on the back of his horse.

"Come on, Jack," she called.

Jack moved slowly towards the knight. It was like a dream.

The knight picked him up, too. He placed Jack on the horse, behind Annie.

The knight got on behind them. He slapped the reins.

The black horse cantered beside the moonlit water of the moat

Jack rocked back and forth in the saddle. The wind blew his hair. He felt very brave and very powerful.

He felt as if he could ride for ever on this horse, with this mysterious knight. Over the ocean. Over the world. Over the moon.

A hawk shrieked in the darkness.

"There's the tree house," said Annie. She pointed towards a grove of trees.

The knight steered the horse towards

the trees.

"See. There it is," Annie said, pointing to the ladder.

The knight brought his horse to a stop. He dismounted and helped Annie down.

"Thank you, sir," she said. And she bowed.

Then Jack. "Thank you," he said. And he bowed also.

The knight got back on his horse. He raised his gloved hand. Then he slapped the reins and rode off through the mist.

Annie climbed up the tall ladder and Jack followed. They climbed into the dark tree house and looked out of the window.

The knight was riding towards the

outer wall. They saw him go through the outer gate.

Clouds started to cover the moon again. For a brief moment, Jack thought he saw the knight's armour gleaming on the top of a hill beyond the castle.

The clouds covered the moon completely. And a black mist swallowed the land.

"He's gone," whispered Annie.

Jack shivered in his wet clothes as he kept staring at the blackness.

"I'm cold," said Annie. "Where's the Pennsylvania book?"

Jack heard Annie fumble in the darkness. He kept looking out of the window.

"I think this is it," said Annie. "I feel a silk bookmark."

Jack was only half-listening. He was hoping to see the knight's armour gleam again in the distance.

"Okay. I'm going to use this," said Annie, "because I think it's the right one. Here goes. Okay. I'm pointing. I'm going to wish. I wish we could go to Frog Creek!"

Jack heard the wind begin to blow. Softly at first.

"I hope I pointed to the right picture in the right book," said Annie.

"What?" Jack looked back at her. "Right picture? Right book?"

The tree house began to rock. The wind got louder and louder.

"I hope it wasn't the dinosaur book!" said Annie.

"Stop!" Jack shouted at the tree house.

Too late.

The tree house started to spin. It was spinning and spinning!

The wind was screaming.

Then suddenly there was silence.

Absolute silence.

10

One Mystery Solved

The air was warm.

It was dawn. Far away a dog barked.

"I think that's Henry barking!" Annie said. "We *did* come home."

They both looked out of the tree house window.

"That was close," said Jack.

In the distance, streetlights lit their street. There was a light on in their upstairs window.

"Uh-oh," said Annie. "I think Mum and Dad are up. Hurry!"

"Wait." In a daze, Jack unzipped his rucksack. He pulled out the castle book. It was quite wet. But Jack placed it back with all the other books.

"Come on! Hurry!" said Annie, scooting out of the tree house.

Jack followed her down the ladder.

They reached the ground and took off between the grey-black trees.

They left the woods and ran down their deserted street.

They got to their garden and crept across the lawn. Right up to the back door.

Jack and Annie slipped inside the house.

"They're not downstairs yet," whispered Annie.

"Shhh," said Jack.

He led the way up the stairs and down

the hall. No sign of his mum or dad. But he could hear water running in the bathroom.

Their house was so different from the dark cold castle. So safe and cosy and friendly.

Annie stopped at her bedroom door. She gave Jack a smile, then disappeared inside her room.

Jack hurried into his room. He took off his damp clothes and pulled on his dry soft pyjamas.

He sat down on his bed and unzipped his rucksack. He took out his wet notebook. He felt around for the pencil, but his hand touched something else.

Jack pulled the blue leather bookmark out of his bag. It must have fallen out of the castle book.

Jack held the bookmark close to his lamp and studied it. The leather was smooth and worn. It seemed ancient.

For the first time Jack noticed a letter on the bookmark. A fancy M.

Jack opened the drawer next to his bed. He took out the gold medallion.

He looked at the letter on it. It was the same M.

Now this was an amazing new fact.

Jack took a deep breath. One mystery solved.

The person who had dropped the gold medallion in the time of the dinosaurs was the same person who owned all the books in the tree house.

Who *was* this person?

Jack placed the bookmark next to the medallion. He closed the drawer.

He picked up his pencil. He turned to the least wet page in his notebook. And he started to write down this new fact.

the sam

But before he could draw the M, his eyes closed.

He dreamed they were with the knight again. All three of them riding the black horse through the cool dark night. Beyond the outer wall of the castle. And up over a moonlit hill.

Into the mist.

MAGIC TREE HOUSE

If you love reading all about Jack and Annie's adventures then you'll want to join the

MAGIC TREE HOUSE CLUB

Members will receive:

* A reading ladder to keep a record of the books you have read. Make sure you save the token below for this.

* A membership card and newsletters.

* Exclusive news and freebies!

To join the club send your full name and address, with the signature of your parent / guardian to:

**The Magic Tree House Club
Publicity Dept, Scholastic Children's Books,
Commonwealth House, 1-19 New Oxford Street,
London WC1A 1NU.**

(membership packs cannot be sent out without a parental signature)

Adventure is waiting inside every Magic Tree House Book!

READING LADDER TOKEN

YOUng HiPPO

More brilliant story books to collect from Young Hippo:

Mermaid's Wish
Unicorn's Wish
The Genie's Wish
Carol Barton

Royal Blunder
Royal Blunder &
the Haunted House
Henrietta Branford

School Poems
Jennifer Curry

Christmas Quackers
Sylvia Green

Broomstick Services
Broomstick Removals
Broomstick Rescues
Broomstick Baby
Ann Jungman

Bobby the Bad
Warlock Watson
What Sadie Saw
Dick King-Smith

Bursting Balloon Mystery
Chocolate Money Mystery
The Bubblegum Tree
The Popcorn Pirates
Alexander McCall Smith

The Ghost in the Telly
Frank Rodgers

Young Hippo Big Books

The Big Book of Dragons
The Big Haunted House Book
The Big Magic Animal Book
The Big Wicked Witch Book
The Big Bad School Bind-Up
The Big Animal Ghost Book